Summer Ice Cream

Written and Illustrated by Dee Smith

Copyright © 2017

Summer ice cream is favorite treat.

So fun to scoop and also to eat.

A treat that most won't want to miss.

A sweet mound of colorful frozen bliss.

Whether strawberry, vanilla or sweet cookie dough,

I do love ice cream. That's what I know!

Whether chocolate, caramel flavored or butter pecan,

Of many flavors, I am a fan!

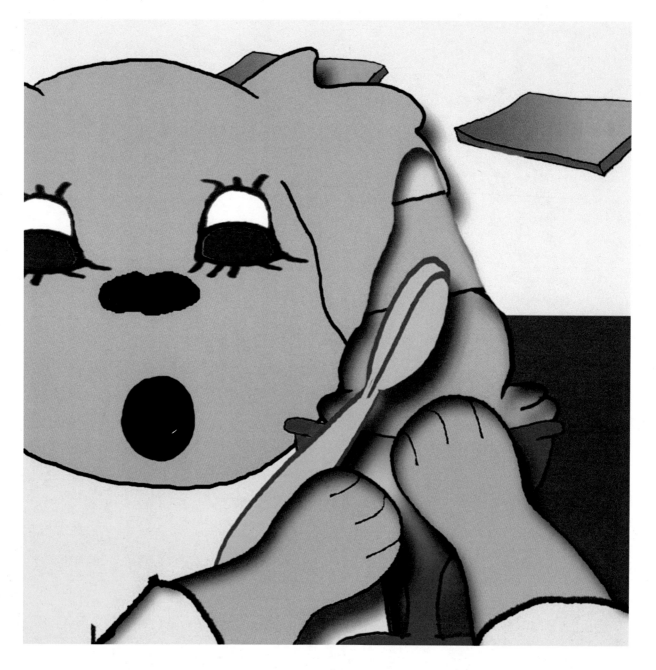

I shape the treat into a mountain with a spoon.

I play with my ice cream but I'll eat it soon!

Summer heat and ice cream are the perfect pair.

Ice cream is great to mix and lovely to share.

Pile it with sprinkles and whipped cream.

**A river of chocolate syrup
shows a gleam.**

With a bright red cherry, it is topped.

My love for ice cream can't be stopped!

Summer ice cream is my favorite treat.

A cool cone on a hot day is hard to beat.

Thank You!

Thank you so much for reading this book.
It means the world to me!
If you liked the book I would much appreciate if you would write a Review on Amazon. I am so thankful for each and every person supporting my dream of being a writer for children. Because you have read this book, yes that means YOU too! Thanks Again!
Stay tuned for more titles on my website Deesignery.com

Regards,
Dee

About the Author:

My name is Dee Smith. I am an Author and Illustrator. My hobbies include graphic design, puppetry, balloon twisting, drawing and of course writing. I am dedicated to my mission of keeping children entertained in fun and innovative ways.

Join Dog on another fun adventure. Take a walk to the harbor!

Read Harbor Next!
A dog walks down to the harbor and describes its vast beauty during a sunny day.

See what the Buzz is all about!
Take a journey to Bee-ville

Read this fun series about a small bee that goes on big adventures and learns along the way!

Made in the USA
Monee, IL
24 July 2022

10237954R00017